James Madison

by
Stuart A. Kallen

BIOGRAPHIES

Founding Fathers

Visit us at
www.abdopub.com

Published by ABDO Publishing Company, 4940 Viking
Drive, Edina, MN 55435. Copyright ©2001 by Abdo
Consulting Group, Inc. International copyrights reserved in
all countries. No part of this book may be reproduced in
any form without written permission from the publisher.

Printed in the United States.

Graphic Design: John Hamilton
Cover Design: MacLean Tuminelly

Cover photo: Corbis
Interior photos and illustrations:
    Corbis, p. 5, 7, 9, 10, 21, 23, 33, 39, 47, 55, 59
    Independence National Historical Park, p. 29, 31
    John Hamilton, p. 15, 25, 41
    National Portrait Gallery, Smithsonian Institution, p. 57
    North Wind Pictures, p. 19, 27, 35, 37, 43, 45, 49, 50, 53
    White House Historical Association, p. 42

   Library of Congress Cataloging-in-Publication Data
Kallen, Stuart A., 1955-
    James Madison / Stuart A. Kallen.
        p. cm. — (The founding fathers)
    Includes index.
    Summary: A biography of the fourth president of the
United States focusing on his role in establishing a new
government for which he is remembered as the Father of the
Constitution.
    ISBN 1-57765-015-8
    1. Madison, James, 1751-1836—Juvenile literature.
2. Presidents—United States—Biography—Juvenile literature.
[1. Madison, James, 1751-1836 2. Presidents.]   I. Title.

E342.K35 2001
973.5'1'092—dc21
[B]
                                        98-004900

Contents

Introduction

J AMES MADISON SAT in the meeting
room at the Philadelphia State House. It
was a hot, muggy day in the summer of
1787. The steaming room was full of
buzzing flies and angry men. This was the room
where the United States of America had been
created in 1776 with the signing of the Declaration
of Independence. But on this day 11 years later,
the United States were not united. Delegates from
every state fought and argued. Some walked out,
never to return.

Madison was one of the delegates from
Virginia. George Washington was another. Day
after day great men like Thomas Jefferson and
Benjamin Franklin gave speeches and wrote
papers. They were facing an awesome task: to
establish a new government for the United States.

*Facing page: A portrait of President James
Madison.*

The old government operated under a set of rules called the Articles of Confederation, but the rules were not working very well. The 13 states were too selfish to work together. The central government was too weak.

All summer long, Madison sat in the front row of the meeting hall. He quietly took notes, even when speeches lasted up to six hours. He wrote down everything—arguments, votes, discussions. At night he went back to his boardinghouse and studied his notes. Then he wrote out his opinions.

Madison had come to the convention with a plan. He wanted a strong central government to rule over the states. Most delegates disagreed with him. As the hot summer wore on, tempers flared and angry voices shook the room. But when the delegates finally signed the Constitution, they were following Madison's plan. His ideas were central to the way the United States would be run. We still follow them today, which is why James Madison is remembered as the Father of the Constitution.

George Washington presiding over the Constitutional Convention at Philadelphia, in 1787.

Life in Virginia

I N THE EARLY 1700s, the colony of
Virginia was ruled by the British
government in far-away England. A few
little towns and villages clung to the coast
of the Atlantic Ocean. To the west lay a vast forest
wilderness where Native Americans lived. In
1716, James Madison's great-grandfather staked
out a 13,500-acre (5,465-hectare) estate in the
Virginia wilderness.

By the time James was born on March 16,
1751, the wild forest had been tamed. It was a
busy plantation with huge fields full of tobacco
and wheat. There were barns, a flour mill,
tobacco-drying sheds, a manor house, and cabins.
The hard work of tobacco farming was done by
slaves. As a boy, James played with the slave
children.

*Facing page: a farm carved out of the Virginia
wilderness.*

Tobacco was Virginia's most important crop. Throughout the Colonies and in Europe people smoked, chewed, and sniffed a kind of tobacco called snuff. The Madisons sent tobacco to England by the shipload. This made their life rich and easy. By 1760, they moved to a bigger, better house. The new Madison home was named Montpelier. In addition to James, the Madisons had four younger sons and daughters.

Above: Montpelier was the family home of President James Madison. The mansion is set amidst the lush green grass and trees of Virginia. Right: In the late eighteenth century, slavery was a way of life in rural Virginia. Tobacco, shown here, was an important crop at the Madison plantation, with most of the hard work done by slaves. Although President Madison wrote of slavery being a great evil, he continued using slaves as laborers until his death in 1836.

Princeton and Politics

JAMES WENT AWAY TO SCHOOL when he was 11. He learned Latin, Greek, algebra, and logic. Madison stayed with his beloved teacher Donald Robertson for five years. After that, Madison's father hired a rector of a nearby church to tutor James for college. After two years, James decided to attend the College of New Jersey at Princeton. It was a surprising choice because New Jersey was a long, hard journey north from Virginia. Most rural southern planters felt uncomfortable in the cities up north.

But Madison fit in perfectly at Princeton. Students were invited to read, debate, and deliver speeches. They were also taught to explain complicated ideas in a simple manner. This was perfect training for a future president. Although Madison was shy, with a weak voice, he worked hard at his studies, so hard that he finished college in two years instead of four.

Facing page: Students at Princeton University.

A young James Madison.

During Madison's college years, politics began to fuel a new fire in America. It started when England began charging taxes on products Americans needed, such as cloth and tea. The English government also set low prices on goods America sold to England, such as flour, lumber, and tobacco.

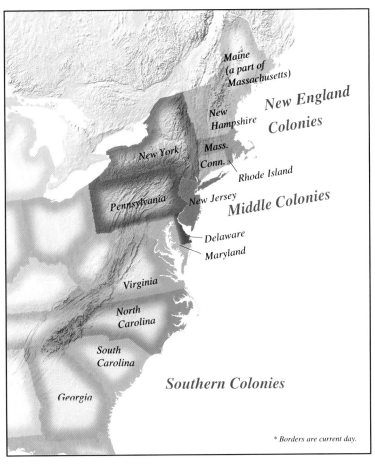

The 13 original American colonies.

The only way Americans could protest the taxes was to boycott, refusing to buy English products. Students at Princeton supported the boycott. Instead of wearing clothes made from fine English broadcloth, they wore coarse, homemade clothes.

Revolutionary War

PEOPLE IN VIRGINIA also supported the boycott. In 1774, Madison and his father were part of a committee that made sure no one broke the boycott. In 1775, war began between England and the colonies.

Madison never actually fought in the Revolutionary War. He joined a local militia and practiced with his rifle. But he was sick much of the time. In fact, doctors did not expect him to live past the age of 30. But he soon felt better thanks to "more activity and less study."

On New Year's Day, 1776, Virginia's English governor fled to a warship in Norfolk Harbor. Then the governor sent soldiers to burn Norfolk. Across Virginia, people picked delegates to set up a new government independent from England. One of those delegates was James Madison.

Madison was one of the youngest of the Virginia delegates. At five feet, six inches tall, he was also the shortest. With his low voice and shy manner, Madison was largely ignored at the convention.

Fighting rages at the Battle of Bunker Hill.
Although James Madison joined a local militia, he
never actually fought in the Revolutionary War.

Taxes and Religion

AT THE VIRGINIA CONVENTION, Madison listened to fiery speeches by politicians. The delegates voted to set up a new state government. It would have a strong legislature elected by the people. The governor would have very weak powers. The delegates did not want one man to rule over them as England's king had done.

The delegate's main problem concerned religion. At the time, most Virginians belonged to the Anglican Church. All taxpayers had to support the church whether they were members or not. Madison thought that having an official state church was the same as "making laws for the human mind." He did not like the idea of giving state tax dollars to one church. He also felt that members of other religions would not be free if there was a state religion. In fact, Baptists were often jailed for their beliefs during this time.

Madison fought against state-sponsored religion, a radical proposal for the time.

Madison set out a proposal that made two points. First, all men should have an equal right to follow their religion. Second, there should be no state religion. This was a radical proposal at the time because almost every government imposed a religion on its people. The convention voted against Madison. He then re-wrote his proposal to say, "All men are equally entitled to the free exercise of religion." This was adopted. Within a year the state did away with the church tax.

How to Pay for a Revolution

AMERICA'S WAR against Britain continued. But there was little money to pay for supplies. General George Washington told America's governing body—the Continental Congress—that the army might "starve, dissolve, or disperse." America's Continental Army was fighting without "shoes, stockings, gloves, or mittens."

To make matters worse, there was no food. The government waited for money from the states, but it never came. In 1781, Washington asked states to send their "ablest, best men to Congress" in Philadelphia to solve the problem. Virginia sent James Madison.

Madison went to the Continental Congress and fought to raise tax money from the states. The Americans also decided to borrow money from France to pay for the war. Later, France sent soldiers to help Americans fight the British. By 1783, the Revolutionary War was over. America was free of British rule.

General George Washington reviews his troops at Valley Forge, Pennsylvania. American soldiers suffered terribly during the winter of 1777-78 because of a lack of food and supplies.

Writing the Constitution

THE WAR WAS WON. But now the states did not want to act together for the common good. Madison went back to the Virginia legislature. He tried to get Virginia to pay taxes to America's federal government. Virginia, along with Connecticut, New Jersey, and Delaware refused to pay their share. In 1786, Virginia sent Madison to a meeting to solve the tax battles between states. Only five of the 13 states sent delegates.

The few delegates decided to call for a Constitutional Convention in May, 1787. The convention would address problems facing the United States. Madison felt this was the last chance to save the country. If they did not come up with a strong federal government, Madison warned that the 13 states, "pulling against each other will soon bring ruin to the whole (country)."

Madison worried that if the 13 states didn't cooperate to create a strong central government, the whole country would be ruined.

Madison wanted a strong government for the whole nation. But he wanted to make sure it did not take away people's freedom. To solve this problem, Madison began reading. He read books about history and government. He read about the ancient Greeks and Romans, who tried democratic government centuries earlier. The Greek and Roman governments fell apart. Madison wanted America to succeed where they had failed.

The Constitutional Convention opened on May 25, 1787. It would last until September 17. During the first days, George Washington was elected convention president. Washington was a well-respected war hero and Madison's fellow Virginia delegate.

Philadelphia's Independence Hall, site of the adoption of the Declaration of Independence and the drafting of the United States Constitution.

The Virginia Plan

MADISON HAD AN IDEA called the Virginia Plan. The states had just fought a war to be free of a strong central government. Madison wanted a government that wouldn't become too strong. But it had to be strong enough to force states to pay their taxes.

Madison's plan divided the central government into three branches. The legislative branch would make laws. This branch would be made up of the House of Representatives and the Senate.

Madison's second branch would be the executive branch, which would carry out the laws made by Congress. This branch would be made up of the president and his cabinet members, such as the Secretary of State.

The third branch would be the judicial branch. This branch would include judges who settled disputes about what the laws meant. Madison's plan called for a country where people voted for their representatives. The representatives voted for the president. And the president appointed the judges.

Madison's Virginia Plan divided the central government into three parts: the legislative, executive, and judicial branches.

Signing the Constitution

SOME OF THE DELEGATES at the convention supported Madison's plan. Others argued against having one man serve as president. They had just gotten rid of England's king and did not want one man with too much power. Other delegates were afraid of giving the vote to the people. They didn't trust the common man to have too much power. (At the time only white men would be allowed to vote.)

After a long debate the delegates adopted Madison's plan for three branches of government. Many delegates agreed to the office of the president under one condition, that George Washington would be elected as first president.

Madison did not agree with every detail of the plan. But he kept working. During that hot summer he gave 161 speeches. By the end of the summer he was proud to put his name on the

Constitution of the United States. Later he wrote,
"The problem to be solved is not what form of
Government is perfect, but which of the forms is
least imperfect."

*George Washington presides at the 1787
Constitutional Convention in Philadelphia. James
Madison stands, quill pen in hand, to
Washington's left.*

The Next Step

ONCE THE INK WAS DRY on the Constitution, nine of the 13 states had to approve, or ratify, it. Then it would become law. To get people to vote for the Constitution, they needed it explained to them. Madison wrote a series of 29 newspaper articles supporting the Constitution. He was joined in his writing by Alexander Hamilton and John Jay. Together the men wrote 51 articles under the pen name "Publius." The whole series of articles was later published as a book called *The Federalist*. This explanation of the Constitution is still considered the best.

Still, many states refused to ratify the Constitution for one reason or another. By spring of 1788, eight states had voted to ratify the document. One more was needed. Madison's own state of Virginia was still debating whether or not to ratify. Madison went to the state house and argued for ratification. After a long, convincing speech, Virginia agreed to ratify the Constitution.

By July every state had ratified except for New York, North Carolina, and Rhode Island. Madison ran for a seat in the House of Representatives and won. On the first day of Congress, Madison argued for a tax on imports. He won, finally giving the national government an income.

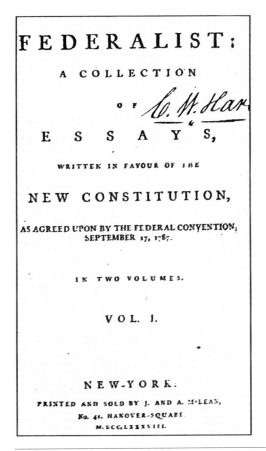

A copy of "The Federalist," written by James Madison, Alexander Hamilton, and John Jay, to convince voters to approve the new Constitution.

The Bill of Rights

MANY PEOPLE were still worried that the new government had too much power. They wanted the Constitution to guarantee people's rights. Madison had hundreds of suggestions from the states' ratifying committees. He reduced them to a list of basic rights, including freedom of religion, freedom of the press, and the right to a trial if accused of a crime. These rights became the first 10 amendments to the Constitution, and are known as the Bill of Rights. When the Bill of Rights was added to the Constitution, the remaining states voted to ratify it.

The new Congress elected George Washington as the first president in February 1789. He was sworn in on April 30 in New York City. The country celebrated with fireworks and speeches.

But Washington was not sure how a president should behave. He asked his old friend James Madison. Madison answered, "The more simple we are in our manners, the more rational dignity we shall acquire."

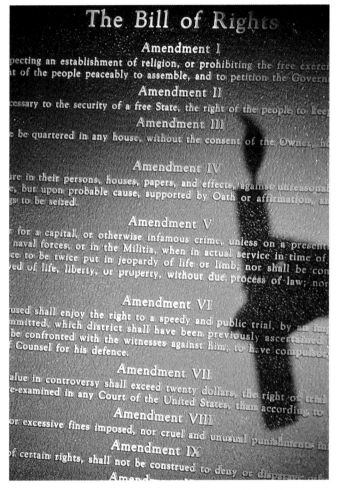

The shadow of a hand holding a candle falls on a bronze version of The Bill of Rights.

Republicans and Federalists

MADISON SPENT the next eight years in the United States House of Representatives. Much like today, the politicians were locked in a constant struggle over ideas. One group called themselves Republicans. They were centered around Madison and Thomas Jefferson. Republicans believed that the central government should be weaker and give states more power.

The other group in Congress was called the Federalists. They centered on the new Secretary of the Treasury Alexander Hamilton. Federalists believed in a strong, powerful federal government to rule over the states.

Federalists were largely northern businessmen who wanted the nation's capital to be located in New York City or Philadelphia. They were

Washington, D.C. in the early 1800s. The inset is of the old Capitol before it burned in 1814.

bankers and merchants who still did business with England. Federalists favored the wealthy. President Washington tended to side with the Federalists.

Republicans were mostly southerners and rural people. They were farmers who did business with France. They wanted a new capital in the South on the Potomac River. Republicans favored the common working person.

Marriage to Dolley

AFTER WASHINGTON served two terms as president, he wanted to retire. Federalist John Adams was elected as the second president of the United States in 1796. With the Republican Party losing power, Madison went back to Virginia. He too wanted to retire, after having served 20 years in politics.

Madison didn't return to Montpelier alone. On September 14, 1794, he married a pretty widow named Dolley Payne Todd. The two partners could not have been more different. Dolley was 17 years younger than James. They were about the same height. James wore simple black suits, and had a stiff manner. Dolley wore big hats with feathers and elegant dresses. She was warm and charming. But the Madisons were happy together.

Madison's retirement did not last long. By 1800, people were fed up with Adams and the Federalists. They elected Thomas Jefferson as president. Jefferson called on his old friend James Madison to serve as Secretary of State. Madison would serve in the nation's new capital, Washington, D.C.

Dolley Madison.

Secretary of State

WHEN THE MADISONS arrived in Washington, D.C. in 1801 all they saw were dirt roads and a few buildings. The Capitol building was only half finished. The president's house, the White House, was in the middle of a muddy field. There were few houses and fewer businesses. As Secretary of State, Madison was expected to entertain diplomats from England, France, and Spain. But restaurants, taverns, and theaters were in short supply.

Right from the beginning, Madison's job was very difficult. England was at war with France. France, which was led by Napoleon Bonaparte, was taking over most of Europe. Madison and Jefferson wanted to stay out of this war. But the Federalists wanted to declare war on France. And the Republicans wanted to declare war—again— on England.

Thomas Jefferson (left) seeking advice from his Secretary of State, James Madison (right).

America's neutrality paid off. France still controlled a large portion of North America, from Louisiana all the way up to modern-day Idaho. This area, called the Louisiana Territory, stretched from the Gulf of Mexico north to Minnesota, and from the Mississippi River to the Rocky Mountains.

Napoleon knew he couldn't fight in Europe and control the Louisiana Territory at the same time. So for only $15 million, the United States purchased the Louisiana Territory. The size of the United States doubled with this one purchase. The Federalists complained that America was paying for a vast "desert." But the Louisiana Purchase made Jefferson and Madison very popular with the common people.

The Louisiana Territory, bought from France for only $15 million, doubled the size of the United States.

Madison the President

O N MARCH 4, 1809, James Madison was sworn in as the fourth president of the United States. Many tough choices lay ahead. The Federalist Party had become very strong again. They opposed Madison at every turn. To make matters worse, Congress was divided. The Republicans controlled the House of Representatives. The Federalists controlled the Senate.

James Madison, president of the United States.

British sailors kidnapping Americans to serve in the British Navy.

War continued between France and England. Both countries attacked American trading ships on the open sea. The British kidnapped American sailors and forced them into the British Navy. Both countries were trying to drag the United States into the war. Madison asked both sides to quit attacking American ships. He promised that America would side with the country that quit first. Finally France agreed. On June 18, 1812, the United States declared war on England.

The War of 1812

THE UNITED STATES acted quickly to capture Canada, which was controlled by the British. A victory there might force Great Britain to end the war. But the U.S. Army was poorly trained. The navy had no ships on the Great Lakes, which are on the border between the United States and Canada. In Detroit, 2,500 Americans surrendered to 700 British without a shot being fired. Other embarrassing losses followed.

Despite the bungled fighting, Madison was elected to a second term in the fall of 1812. The Federalists were against the war with England. They refused to raise taxes to fight the war. Madison had to borrow millions to pay the soldiers. To make matters worse, Federalist businessmen made millions on black-market (illegal) trade with Britain.

Facing page: British ships blockading Chesapeake Bay.

The Federalist actions seriously harmed the war effort. Madison became very sick in the summer of 1813. And the British fought on.

The Americans were beginning to win a few battles. With only 25 ships the U.S. Navy beat back Britain's 700 warships. A few months later General William Henry Harrison pushed the British out of the Michigan Territory. Americans also fought and won in the Northeast.

In 1814, the British and French made peace. But the British were eager to punish America for its role in the war. Thousands of tough, seasoned British soldiers were sent to America. At just that time, Madison wanted to stop the war with England. He sent negotiators to England to work out a peace treaty. But England refused to make peace.

Cannon batteries line the defensive walls at Fort McHenry, the guardian of the harbor at Baltimore, Maryland. During the War of 1812, American defenders withstood a 25-hour attack by British forces on September 13-14, 1814. The battle inspired poet Francis Scott Key to write "The Star-Spangled Banner."

Washington Burns

THE BRITISH WERE getting ready to invade Washington, D.C. President Madison ordered 10,000 militiamen to defend the capital city. But Madison's Secretary of War stalled. The city had no defense. There were no roadblocks, no ammunition, and no militiamen.

In August 1814, 50 British ships dropped anchor in Virginia. Two days later 4,000 British soldiers marched on Washington, D.C. No one tried to stop them. On August 24, a messenger woke up James and Dolley Madison. The British were invading. Madison rode out to help the militia defend the city.

British troops looting and burning the lightly defended Washington, D.C.

British Commander George Cockburn orders his men to burn the White House.

The president found tired, inexperienced soldiers. They were spread out in different areas with no plan. Madison rode back behind the lines. He said, "the militia ran like sheep chased by dogs." At the White House, Dolley tried to save what she could.

The Madisons planned an escape across the Potomac. British Commander George Cockburn invaded the White House. He broke open a liquor cabinet and jokingly drank a toast to James Madison. After he ate dinner, Cockburn ordered his men to start a fire at every window in the White House.

As Madison rode away from the capital that night he saw "columns of flame and smoke ascending throughout the night... from the Capitol, the President's house, and other public edifices... some burning slowly, others with bursts of flame and sparks mounting high up."

Three days later the British left. Madison returned to a city that was reduced to smoking ashes. The only buildings untouched were the Post Office and the Patent Office. The British left private homes alone, so President Madison and the first lady moved in with relatives.

Victory Over Britain

AFTER THE BURNING of Washington, D.C., Madison refused to leave the city even though the British were still nearby. Congress used the Post Office and Patent Office to meet. Other officials worked from home. The British were turned back in New York and Baltimore. After watching the fight at Baltimore's Fort McHenry, Francis Scott Key wrote the Star Spangled Banner. The song later became America's national anthem.

The British switched their strategy to the south. Madison asked Congress for $50 million to continue fighting. The Federalists would not release the money. Finally, the Americans defeated the British in New Orleans on January 8, 1815. On February 14, the British agreed to a peace treaty.

On February 17, Madison announced the war was over. Everyone was happy, except for the Federalists. Jefferson wrote that their disloyalty would have gotten them hanged for treason in any other country. But, he wrote, "We let them live as the laughing stocks of the world."

The ruins of the Capitol building after British forces burned Washington, D.C.

Back to Montpelier

AFTER THE WAR OF 1812, Madison's second term was almost over. The war had taught Americans that they needed a strong fighting force at all times. Congress easily passed a bill to form a permanent army and navy. War taxes were used to pay off the national debt. Madison's good friend James Monroe was elected president in 1816.

After Monroe's inauguration in 1817, the Madisons stayed in Washington for a month of farewell celebrations. Finally, they left for Montpelier. The nation had changed a great deal since Madison first entered public life. Instead of riding a carriage home, the Madisons rode on a new form of transportation—the steamboat.

After serving two terms as president, James Madison retired to his home at Montpelier, Virginia.

A Gentleman's Life—and Death

BACK AT MONTPELIER, the Madisons had a steady stream of visitors. Madison became a gentleman farmer. Although he was retired, he was still called upon for advice. President Monroe sent him official documents to read. Politicians wrote him and asked for his help.

In 1829, Virginia called on Madison to help write a new state constitution. Once again, Madison was a delegate at the Virginia Constitutional Convention. He was the only man there who in 1776 had been at the original convention—53 years earlier. The delegates cheered the elder statesman, and they lined up to shake his hand.

By 1831, rheumatism had stiffened the former president. He found writing difficult and could only move his fingertips. Madison began putting his papers in order. Historians visited him to ask about the founding of the United States.

Madison had outlived all his friends. Jefferson had died on July 4, 1826. On July 4, 1831, James Monroe died in New York. Madison wrote, "Having outlived so many of my contemporaries, I ought not to forget that I may be thought to have outlived myself."

Madison's health grew worse. People said he should try to hang on until the Fourth of July. That's the date that Adams, Jefferson, and Monroe had all died. But Madison could not hang on. He died at the age of 85 on June 28, 1836.

James Madison in his late 70s, about the time he attended a convention to help rewrite the Virginia constitution.

Conclusion

THE ENTIRE NATION mourned when James Madison passed away. Through his vision and genius he had formed a new kind of nation, one that survives to this very day. Madison nurtured the birth of America, from the Continental Congress to the White House. He always believed in the ideals put forth in the Constitution. He saw the nation struggle during the Revolutionary War, and again during the War of 1812. In war and in peace, James Madison will always be remembered as the Father of the Constitution.

Facing page: An aging President James Madison, painted in the 1820s.

Timeline

March 16, 1751	James Madison born in Virginia.
1760	Madison family moves to mansion at Montpelier.
1771	Graduates from College of New Jersey (now Princeton University).
1776	Member of Virginia Constitutional Convention.
1780-83	Member of Continental Congress.
1784-86	Member of Virginia Legislature.
1787	Member of Constitutional Convention.
1789-97	Member of U.S. House of Representatives.
Sept. 14, 1794	Marries Dolley Paine Todd.
1801-1809	Secretary of State under President Thomas Jefferson.
1803	Louisiana Purchase from France doubles size of United States.
1809-1817	President of the United States.
1812-1815	War of 1812.
August 1814	British burn Washington, D.C.
1817	Madison retires to Montpelier, Virginia.
1829	Attends Virginia Constitutional Convention.
June 28, 1836	James Madison dies at Montpelier.

Where on the Web?

American Presidents Life Portraits

http://www.americanpresidents.org/presidents/
president.asp?PresidentNumber=4

The Federalist Papers

http://www.mcs.net/~knautzr/fed/madison.htm

Infoplease: Dolley Madison

http://kids.infoplease.lycos.com/ce6/people/
A0831072.html

Internet Public Library

http://www.ipl.org/ref/POTUS/jmadison.html

Montpelier, Home of James Madison

http://www.montpelier.org/

Mr. President: Profiles of our Nation's Leaders

http://web7.si.edu/president/gallery/
detail.cfm?prez_ID=4

Glossary

American Revolution: the war between Great Britain and its American colonies that lasted from 1775 to 1783. America won its independence in the war.

Bill of Rights: a statement of citizen's rights that make up the first 10 amendments to the United States Constitution. Some of the amendments guarantee free speech, protection from search and seizure, and the right of a militia to bear arms.

boycott: to try to change the actions of a company or government by refusing to buy their products.

The Colonies: the British territories that made up the first 13 states of the United States. The 13 colonies were the states of New Hampshire, Massachusetts, Rhode Island, Connecticut, New York, New Jersey, Pennsylvania, Delaware, Maryland, Virginia, North Carolina, South Carolina, and Georgia.

Constitution: the document that spells out the principles and laws that govern the United States.

Constitutional Convention: the meeting of men who wrote the United States Constitution.

Continental Army: the army that fought the British in the Revolutionary War.

Continental Congress: lawmakers who governed the 13 colonies after they declared their independence from Great Britain.

Declaration of Independence: the document written by Thomas Jefferson that declared America's independence from Great Britain.

Federalist: a political party that favors a strong central government over the states.

House of Representatives: a governing body elected by popular vote to rule a nation.

legislature: a body of persons with the power to make, change, or repeal laws.

militia: a body of citizens enrolled in military service during a time of emergency.

ratify: to express approval of a document, such as the United States Constitution.

Index